This 1989 edition published by Derrydale Books,
distributed by Crown Publishers, Inc.,
225 Park Avenue South
New York, N.Y. 10003

Directed by HELENA Productions Ltd.
Illustrated by Van Gool-Lefevre-Loiseaux

Produced by Twin Books
15 Sherwood Place
Greenwich, CT 06830
Printed in Spain by
Printer Industria gráfica sa. Barcelona
D. L. B.: 26784-1989
ISBN 0-517-69315-1

hgfedcba

The Ugly Duckling

DERRYDALE BOOKS
New York

Twin Books

One warm spring morning, after Mother Duck had been sitting on her nest of eggs for some weeks, she heard a *tap! tap! tap!* Soon her ducklings pecked and scratched their way out of the eggs. They looked about and blinked their big eyes at the bright light.

"Welcome to the world," said Mother Duck gently. "I am your mother!"

The little yellow ducklings quacked excitedly to each other in their tiny voices. The last duckling was still struggling out of his shell. He emerged, much larger than the others, craned his long neck and gave a loud honk.

"Goodness!" exclaimed Mother Duck. The smaller ducklings looked at each other with surprise. The last duckling was gray and gawky. A bit of shell still clung to the top of his head. The long silence was broken by a shrill giggle from one of the ducklings.

Soon they were all laughing and pointing unkindly at the ugly duckling.

The other barnyard fowl came to see what all the laughter was about. They, too, stared at the ugly duckling. Then the rooster crowed his disapproval.

The other ducks jeered. "You're a disgrace to us ducks!" one of them said.

The ugly duckling huddled under his mother's wing. "You should be ashamed of yourselves," quacked his mother angrily, "picking on a helpless little duckling. Leave him alone!"

11

But the commotion only got worse, as the turkey and other ducks and chickens joined the squabble. "He's got to go!" they honked and clucked and quacked. Not even the ugly duckling's mother could protect him.

The ugly duckling found an opening in the wall and fled across the meadow. The loud birds followed him a short distance. Then he could hear their angry voices as he darted under the fence and stumbled into the forest.

The ugly duckling was afraid. Was it his fault that he didn't look like the others? Before long he noticed that the forest was growing darker and colder. "I'll just have to take care of myself," he said. He made a grassy nest under a big tree, and passed his first long night alone, trying not to think of his mother's soft feathers and kind eyes.

The ugly duckling awoke shivering with
the cold. He felt lonely and hungry and
not at all brave. He began to cry.

Suddenly, he heard voices. A couple of field mice had come to see who was sobbing.

"Hi, there," said the bigger mouse. "I'm Tim and this here's Tom. We want to know what a little thing like you is doing out here by yourself."

As the duckling told his sad story, Tom wrapped his scarf around the duckling's neck to keep him warm.

"Maybe you could be friends with that fella over there," suggested Tom, pointing to a heron in a nearby pond.

"I'll give it a try," responded the ugly duckling doubtfully. He waddled to the water's edge.

The heron greeted the ugly duckling with an unfriendly glare, then hopped up on the bank. His legs were so long that he loomed over the duckling, who turned and fled.

"What you need," said Tim, "is to be with your own kind." He and Tom urged the duckling toward the ducks in a nearby pond.

But when the duckling approached the strange ducks, he was not greeted warmly. The ducklings jeered at him, and the big duck splashed him, quacking, "Go away!"

Crestfallen, the ugly duckling paddled back to the shore. "No one likes me because I'm so ugly," he said sadly.

"There now," comforted Tim. "I've already got a solution to your problem." He winked at Tom and pointed to a little farmhouse in a clearing.

The mice urged the duckling to the farmhouse door, promising a warm, dry place to sleep and lots to eat.

Sure enough, when the farmer's wife came out to milk the cow...

...she scooped up the ugly duckling. "Are you lost?" she asked gently, and brought him into the house.

The duckling slept in a basket that
night and had scraps of bread to eat in the
morning. But as the days and weeks
passed, he felt more and more uneasy in
the small house. He longed to swim on the
water and feel the breeze ruffle his
feathers. He missed his friends the mice,
who sometimes came to peek at him
through the window.

One day, when the farmer's wife opened the door, the duckling rushed out. "Let's go!" he quacked, and the three friends ran across the meadow.

They played tag on the lakeshore, but the duckling had an unfair advantage because he could swim. That night the duckling found a bush to sleep under, and the mice slept in their burrows.

And so the days of summer passed. The duckling stopped wishing for his own kind, feeling happy by himself or with the mice. Soon it was autumn, and the lake echoed with gunshots as hunting season opened. Many geese and ducks were shot, but the ugly duckling escaped by hiding with the mice.

The birds began flying south, and once the ugly duckling felt a strange longing when he saw three beautiful white birds pass silently overhead.

Winter came as suddenly as the snow one night, and in the morning laughter rang through the air as the ugly duckling and the mice slid down a hill, and shook snow off the trees onto each other. The woods and the meadow looked beautiful cloaked in white, but winter was not so much fun later that day, when it turned bitterly cold.

The three friends decided they had to
seek warmth to survive. The wind blew
at them as they trudged through the snow.

Suddenly Tim shouted, "Look! The farmhouse!" But just
at that moment the duckling collapsed in the snow, and the
mice couldn't rouse him.

"We've got to get help fast," said Tom, "before he freezes.
Quick, run and get the barn mice."

Tim scrambled to the barn, and before long he returned
with helpers.

The mice heaved and pulled and pushed the duckling through the snow, until at last they managed to get him into the barn.

"Over here!" squeaked one of the barn mice. "That's it! Easy does it!"

Tim and Tom were afraid that their friend might never awaken. Lovingly, they made him a nest of straw, and huddled close to him through the long night, patting his feathers with their little paws.

Light slowly filtered into the barn as
morning came, and suddenly the duckling
raised his head. "Where am I?" he asked.
Cheers filled the barn as the mice
shouted with joy.

The duckling listened intently as the mice explained what had happened. "You're the best friends a duck could have," he said to Tim and Tom. "And thanks," he added to the barn mice.

The friends decided to spend the rest of the winter in the barn. They passed the days playing charades and hide-and-seek.

37

When spring came the duckling yearned again for the woods and the lake. Tim and Tom thought of their snug burrows near the lakeshore.

One day they decided to return to the lake. They thanked the barn mice for their help and friendship and set off across the meadow, waving goodbye.

When the friends slipped under the fence at the edge of the farm, the ugly duckling suddenly began to cry.

"What is it?" asked Tom. The duckling had remembered the birds he had seen flying south in the fall. They were graceful and white, and all winter their beauty had haunted him. When he told the mice, they tried to cheer him up. "Those were swans you saw," said Tim. "They should be back any day now. I'm sure they'll want you to join them."

But the ugly duckling felt sure that no bird as beautiful and proud as the swans would welcome him, and he only felt worse.

Just then they heard a honking overhead, and looked up to see the swans circling over the lake. The beautiful creatures alighted on the water.

"Come over here!" cried Tom to the duckling. "I've got something to show you."

The duckling joined the mice at the water's edge. At their insistence, he peered at his reflection, and suddenly caught his breath.

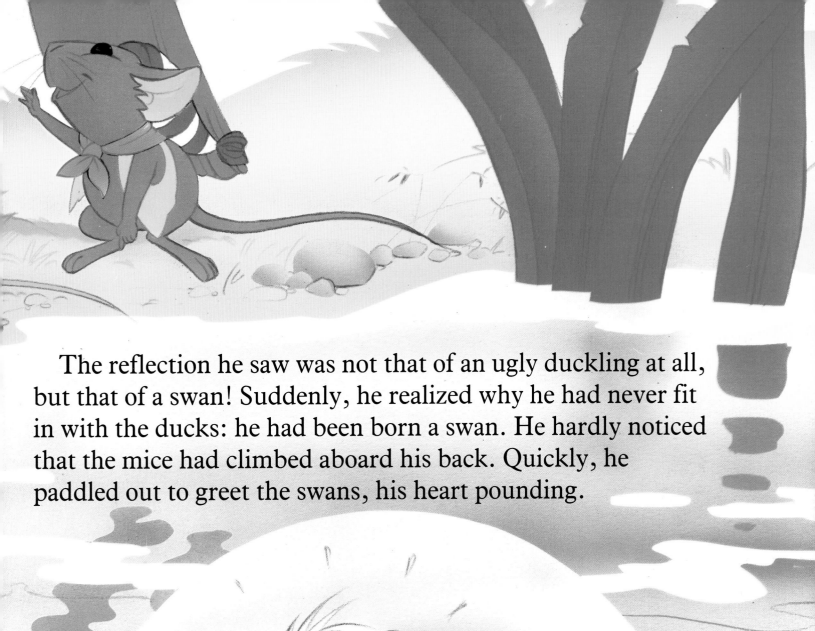

The reflection he saw was not that of an ugly duckling at all, but that of a swan! Suddenly, he realized why he had never fit in with the ducks: he had been born a swan. He hardly noticed that the mice had climbed aboard his back. Quickly, he paddled out to greet the swans, his heart pounding.

The other swans stared with surprise when he approached, and the ugly duckling prepared himself for their jeering. As they stretched their long necks toward him, he expected the worst, but instead, they stroked his feathers with their bills, accepting him as one of their own. No one was happier at that moment than the duckling's devoted friends—except, perhaps, the once ugly duckling himself, who had turned into the most beautiful swan of all.